D1477353

A catalogue record for this book is available from the British Library

Published by Ladybird Books Ltd
27 Wrights Lane London W8 5TZ
A Penguin Company

LADYBIRD and the device of a Ladybird are trademarks of Ladybird Books Ltd
TARZAN™ Owned by Edgar Rice Burroughs, Inc. And used by permission.

© (1999) Edgar Rice Burroughs, Inc. and Disney Enterprises, Inc.

Printed and bound in Great Britain by
Butler & Tanner Ltd, Frome and London

Ladybird

Kala the gorilla was puzzled. She could hear a baby crying high up in a strange tree house. She knew that this baby needed help. So she crossed the rope bridge that linked the tree house to the jungle.

Peering into the tree house, Kala saw signs of a
fight. She stopped, but the baby was still crying.
So she followed the sound of the baby's cry to a
cradle. Inside was an odd-looking, hairless baby.
As Kala picked him up the baby smiled up at her.

7

Suddenly a terrifying roar shook the tree house. It was Sabor the leopard! The vicious cat had already taken Kala's own son, and now it wanted this baby too.

Kala held the little boy tightly and jumped to the ground. Then she took him safely to her home.

Kala decided to adopt the little boy. But Kerchak, the leader of the gorillas, refused to have anything to do with him.

Nevertheless, Kala still insisted that she would keep the baby and she named him Tarzan.

As he grew, Tarzan realised how different he was from the rest of his family. The other gorillas nicknamed him 'the hairless wonder'.

Tarzan had many friends, but his best friend was a gorilla called Terk. Tarzan followed her everywhere, and he did anything she asked.

One day Terk dared Tarzan to fetch a hair from one of the elephants at the waterfalls. She thought Tarzan would be too scared, and that he would go back to Kala. But she was wrong. Tarzan leapt off the cliff into the water.

In the lagoon below, a young elephant named Tantor saw
Tarzan's shape in the water and screamed. Then Tarzan
grabbed one of the elephants' tails. Tarzan was thrown high
into the air and landed with a splash. The elephants were
terrified and stampeded towards the gorillas' home.

The gorillas rushed to the lagoon, wondering what had caused the stampede. Kerchak blamed Tarzan at once. "You do not belong here!" he shouted.

Tarzan ran away. He sat looking at his reflection in a pool of water. "Why am I so different?" he asked himself.

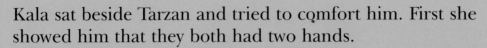

Kala sat beside Tarzan and tried to comfort him. First she showed him that they both had two hands.

"Now," she said, "forget what you see. What do you feel?" And she placed Tarzan's head against her heart. "See? Inside we're the same. Kerchak just can't see that," she told him.

Encouraged, Tarzan promised, "I'll make him see it! I'll be the best ape ever!"

As time passed, Tarzan grew tall and strong. He learned many skills from the animals in the jungle. But he would never befriend Sabor.

One day, the leopard attacked the gorillas and injured Kerchak. Now it was Tarzan's turn to defend his family. Sabor leapt on Tarzan and they tumbled into a deep pit. The apes listened to the sounds of snarling and roaring. Then there was silence.

Tarzan climbed triumphantly out of the pit. He was holding Sabor's body above his head. Solemnly he laid the body at Kerchak's feet.

The gorillas cheered. But their celebrations were stopped by the sound of a gunshot. Kerchak knew that this meant danger and he urged his family to flee deep into the jungle.

But the strange sound only made Tarzan curious. He slipped through the trees and, peering down, he saw three creatures. He'd never seen anything like them before!

They were humans – Professor Porter and his daughter Jane had come to Africa to study gorillas. The third person was their guide, a hunter called Clayton.

As Tarzan watched them, Jane stopped to sketch a baby baboon. Her father and Clayton walked on. The baby snatched Jane's picture and ran away with it. Jane rushed to get the picture back, but the baboon family were angry and they started to chase her.

Jane was terrified, but Tarzan came to her rescue. He carried her away to safety.

Tarzan was curious about Jane. He matched his hand to hers. They were the same! Then Tarzan began to repeat Jane's words, and soon they learnt each other's names.

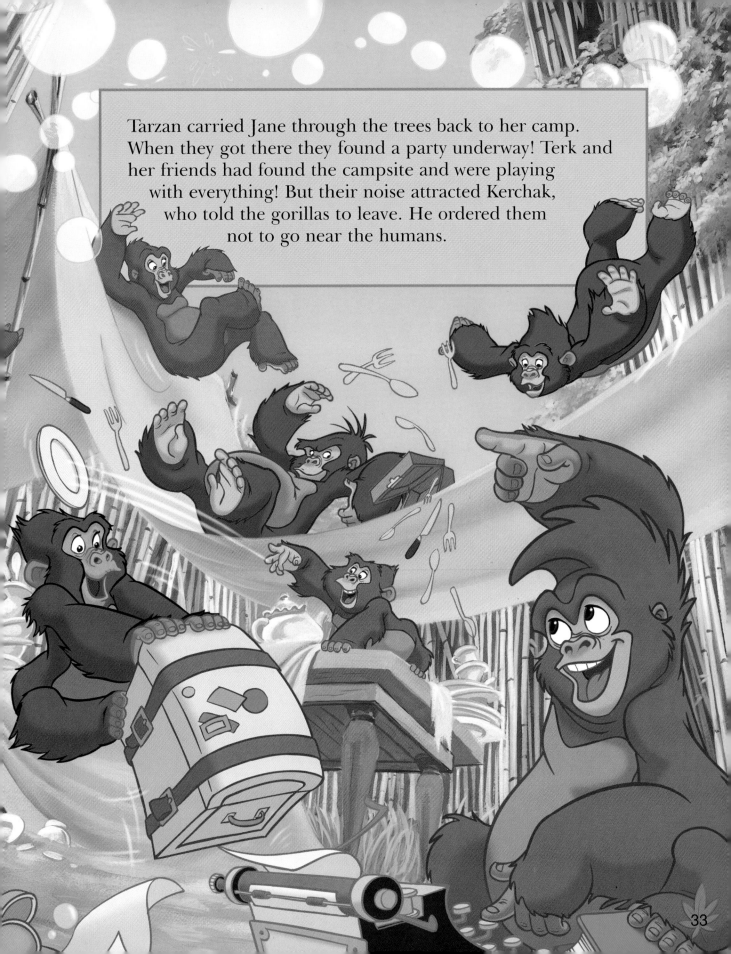

Tarzan carried Jane through the trees back to her camp.
When they got there they found a party underway! Terk and
her friends had found the campsite and were playing
with everything! But their noise attracted Kerchak,
who told the gorillas to leave. He ordered them
not to go near the humans.

When Professor Porter and Clayton returned to the camp, Jane tried to describe her meeting with Tarzan. She was sketching a picture of him when suddenly Tarzan dropped down from a tree – living proof of Jane's strange story. Tarzan was fascinated by the humans, so Jane showed him some scenes of the world outside the jungle.

Tarzan and Jane spent lots of time together, and they quickly became good friends. Tarzan learned more about Jane's world and he showed her round the jungle. But Tarzan refused to take her to the gorillas. And he would only say "Kerchak," when she asked him why.

One day, Tarzan arrived at the camp to find that the Porters were packing to return to England. Tarzan asked Jane not to go, but Jane wouldn't answer. Clayton said slyly, "If only Jane could have spent more time with the gorillas…"

So, hoping that Jane would stay, Tarzan agreed to take them to the gorillas.

Terk and Tantor tricked Kerchak to get him away from the area, and then Jane and Professor Porter made friends with the apes. Clayton too was delighted—but for other reasons. He intended to capture the gorillas.

Suddenly Kerchak returned. He was furious and got ready to attack. Against all he had been taught, Tarzan held Kerchak back to give the humans time to escape.

Kerchak's fury at Tarzan's disobedience was clear. "I asked you to protect our family. And you have betrayed us all," he said. Kala saw her son's pain and knew that she had to show him the tree house. With a heavy heart she led him there and showed him the portrait of his real parents and himself as a baby.

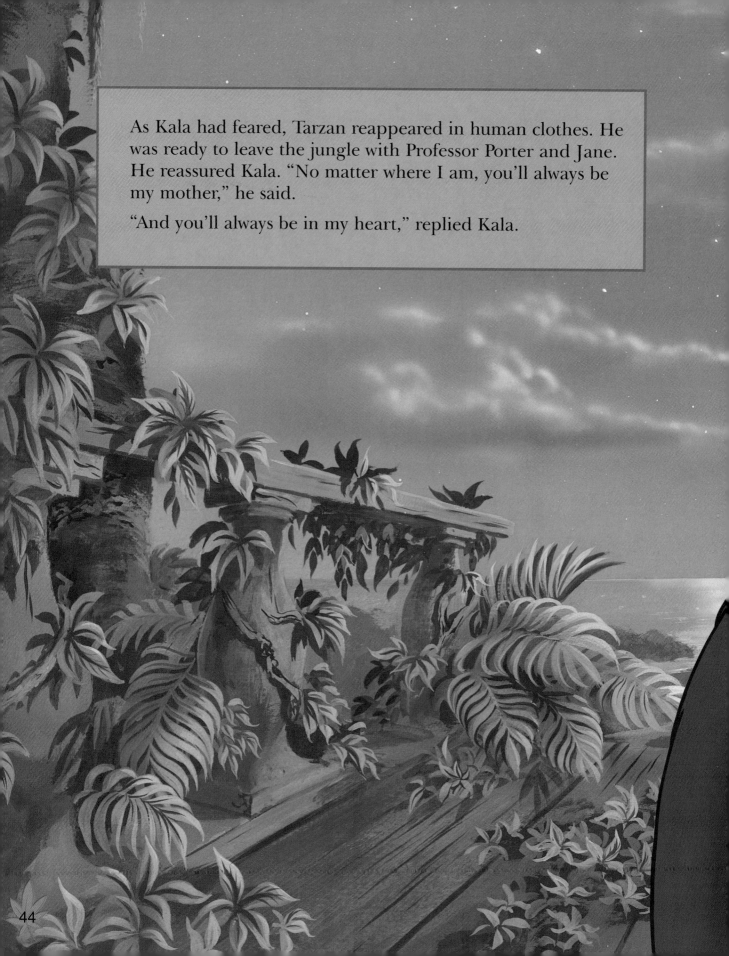

As Kala had feared, Tarzan reappeared in human clothes. He was ready to leave the jungle with Professor Porter and Jane. He reassured Kala. "No matter where I am, you'll always be my mother," he said.

"And you'll always be in my heart," replied Kala.

Jane and Professor Porter were overjoyed that Tarzan would be joining them, and soon they had boarded the ship that would take them to England. Looking back at the jungle, Tarzan said farewell to his old life. He didn't know that he and the Porters had walked straight into Clayton's trap.

Clayton had taken over the ship. He overpowered Tarzan and revealed his real plan to capture the gorillas and sell them. "And it's all thanks to you, Tarzan," Clayton sneered.

Tarzan's cry of despair echoed round the jungle. His animal friends knew that he was in trouble. So they raced to the rescue!

Meanwhile, in the ship's hold, Tarzan blamed himself. "I betrayed my family," he moaned. "Kerchak was right."

Just then, there was a huge crash, as Tantor broke through the deck. Tarzan leapt out to freedom and rushed to stop Clayton!

Clayton's men had already captured most of the apes. Even the great Kerchak was trapped in a corner. Clayton raised his gun and aimed it at Kerchak.

But then Tarzan arrived. Clayton was furious and turned the gun towards Tarzan.

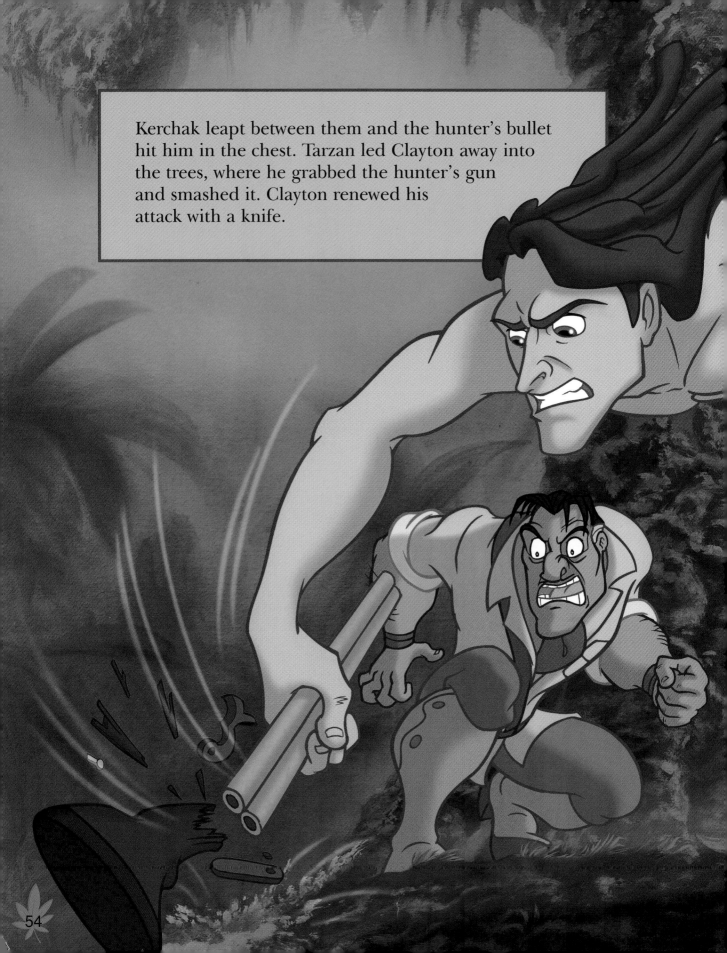

Kerchak leapt between them and the hunter's bullet hit him in the chest. Tarzan led Clayton away into the trees, where he grabbed the hunter's gun and smashed it. Clayton renewed his attack with a knife.

Slashing wildly at the vines, Clayton lunged at Tarzan. But a vine was twisted around his neck and he fell. He would never threaten the apes again.

Tarzan returned to Kerchak's side and pleaded for his forgiveness.

"No. Forgive *me* for not understanding you," Kerchak replied. "Take care of our family… my son."

Some time later, Tarzan and Jane said goodbye on the shore. Professor Porter was waiting for her in a boat. Jane didn't want to leave, and when her father saw how unhappy she was he pointed at Tarzan and said, "Go on, stay! You love him."

And then Professor Porter decided to stay too. Tarzan and the gorillas were delighted. Now they could all live happily in peace ever after.